Which is my dinner?

By Liza Fenech

Which is my dinner?

This book is dedicated to my amazing husband. His loving support has made all the difference.

Help the animals choose which food is right for them!

Do bunnies eat pizza?
Do kitties eat leaves?

Help the animals select the food that is right for them. Then, turn the page and see them enjoying a meal!

Parents, this book will help your child build vocabulary, develop reasoning skills, and have fun in the process!

The dog is hungry.
Help him decide which
food is right for him.

Now, turn the page and see him
munching away on his dinner!

Good job!

Sell your books at
sellbackyourBook.com!
Go to sellbackyourBook.com
and get an instant price
quote. We even pay the
shipping - see what your old
books are worth today!

Inspected By:yesica

00011476340

6340

0001147

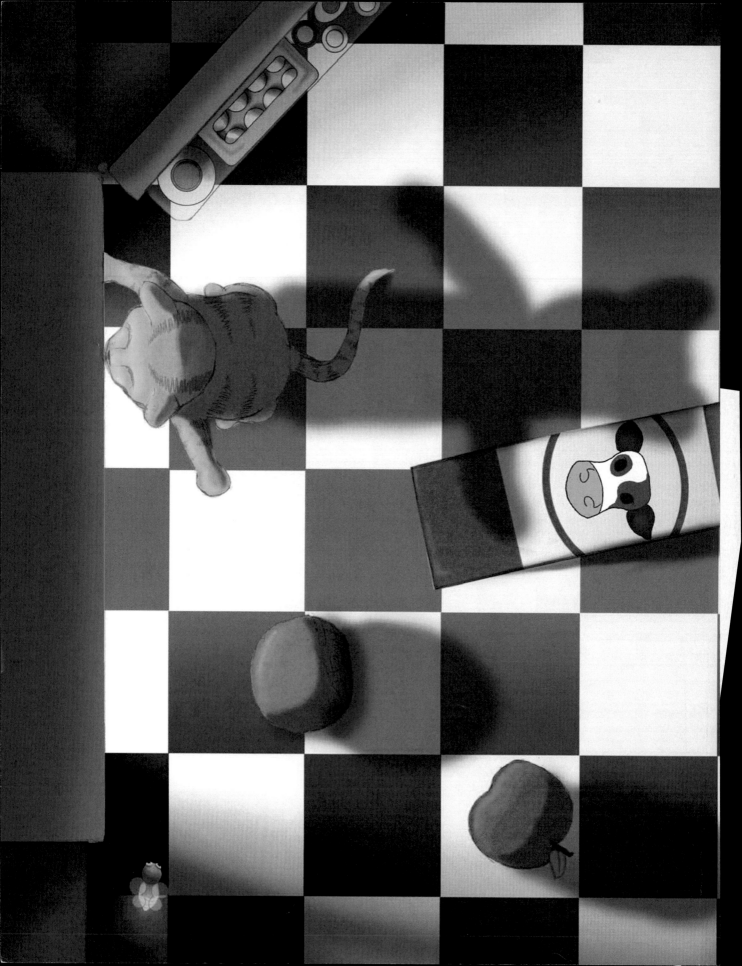

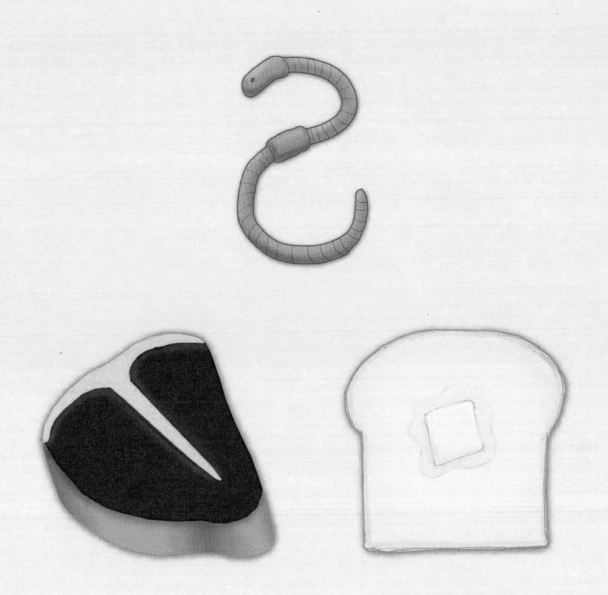

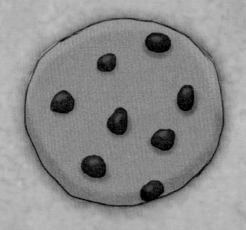

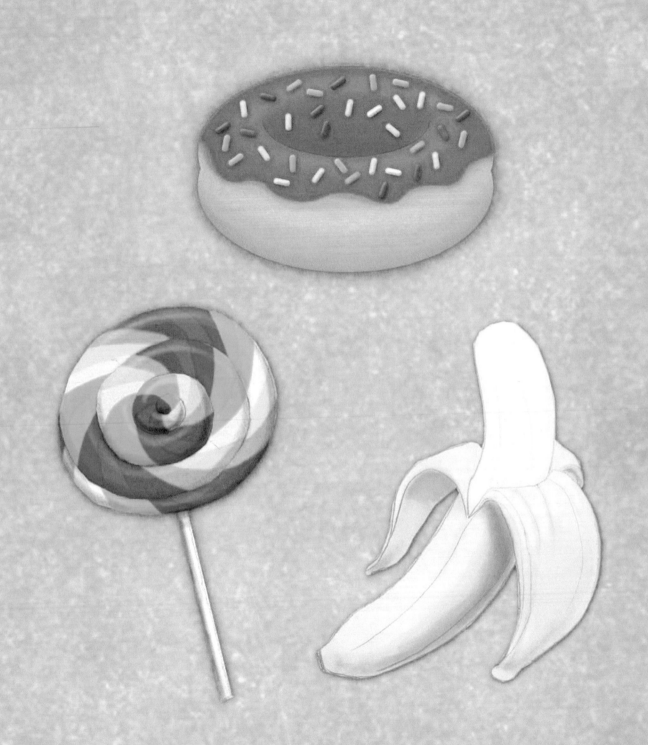

The

For more, check out

PuddleDuckPress.com
or
find us on Amazon.com
by searching for
Liza Fenech.